Ninja Farts

Silent But Deadly!

J.B. O'Neil

Published by J.J Fast Publishing, LLC

Ninja Farts

Silent But Deadly!

Table of Contents

For my son Joe, who loves to laugh about completely disgusting stuff like boogers, farts, Dutch ovens, wet willies, skid marks, ETC...Enjoy!

FREE BONUS – Ninja Farts Audiobook

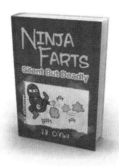

Hey gang…If you'd like to listen to an audiobook version of Ninja Farts while you follow along with this book, you can download it for free for a limited time by going online and copying this link: http://funnyfarts.net/

Enjoy!

A Crazy, Stinky Dream...

Oh no! There are so many enemy ninjas chasing me. I started jumping from tree to tree, leaping so fast that the forest was turning into a green blur. I need to think of something fast!

I am ninja, what do ninjas do in this situation? They remember their teachings. My master always told me the way of the ninja is to be as sneaky as possible, but when that doesn't work create a fart cloud so smelly and thick that nobody could possibly follow you. So that's what I did.

As I ran, I focused all of my energy into making the stinkiest, smelliest, most eye-watering nose-burning butt rocket I could. I flew forward on my green fart jet leaving the other ninjas gagging. I could hear them coughing and yelling to each other—

BEEP BEEP BEEP BEEP!

Why I Hate My Alarm Clock

Ugh, stupid alarm clock. That was the best dream I'd ever had.

"Milo! Milo!" That was my mom calling me.

"Milo!" She was making sure I was awake. Isn't that what alarms are for?

"I'm awake!" I yelled back. My room smelled terrible. I must have been sleep farting again. I guess if you fart in your dreams you fart in real life. I got out of bed and got dressed for school. Mom would be mad if I was late again. The problem was that my stomach was making some gurgling noises. I guess I didn't quite get all the farts out in my dream. I farted so loud and powerfully that I flew down my stairs.

I Blame My Mom

"Milo, you know how I feel about farting." My mom said. "Farting is gross and rude and you should stop doing it." My mom doesn't understand.

"Mom, I can't just *stop* farting. I have to fart. It's who I am." She's a mom, it's not her fault that she doesn't get it.

I sat down at the table and waited for breakfast. She brought me a plate full of eggs and beans. My mom really doesn't get it.

15

The Bully on the Bus

I ate my breakfast and went outside to wait for the bus. My stomach was already telling me that this was going to be a farty day. I just hoped Bobby Buttz-Cratcher wasn't there. He was the meanest kid I knew.

I got on the bus as it pulled up and, oh boy, Bobby was there. Farting. He actually grabbed another kid's face and farted into it so hard that Bobby flew into his seat. He left a fart trail floating in the air behind him, sort of like a shooting star. It was beautiful in a gross green-fart-trail kind of way. The poor kid who got his face farted into was completely knocked out with his head in a gas cloud.

Weird Science Class

We finally got to school. My day always starts with science class. Science and Bobby. It's a good thing science is so cool, because this teacher is so boring.

The class was full of beakers filled with bubbling chemicals and strange fumes floating out of the tops of most of them, but we were all stuck listening to Mr. Figgins drone on and on about something. I didn't really know. He was too boring to listen to. I started getting so sleepy listening to him, but I don't even think he noticed what us kids were doing anyway. He just loved to talk.

Can't Stay Awake...zzzzz

I could feel my eyelids getting heavy sitting at my desk. School is so boring sometimes that no matter how hard I try I just can't stay awake. I don't think teachers will ever understand. Then, just as I was falling asleep, I heard Bobby say something to the kid next to him.

"It's finally done. I've figured out the perfect recipe for my farts. I've been working on them for months in science class and now they're done! These farts that I've made smell so bad that they'll burn your nose-hair out! No one will be able to stand them."

Me...Ninja Fart Master!

Even that news couldn't keep me awake today though. I felt myself fall into the dream world, where I was once again a ninja, this time standing outside a giant castle. I had to get inside and I had to go unseen, as ninjas must.

This fortress seemed impossible to get into, but there were no walls that could keep this fart ninja out. I snuck up to the front gate, hidden by the dark night.

The Terrible Fart King

There was a group of armed guards at the front, making sure nobody got in or out. I ran up the walls and jumped over the guards and made my way to the throne room. When I got there I saw King Bobby Buttz-Cratcher sitting in his throne yelling at his subjects.

"I need more farts! My people aren't paying the fart tax! How is my kingdom supposed to function without the farts?"

Bobby slammed his hands on his throne and stood up. He pointed at a frail old man who was on his knees, "Where are my farts, you? You're late on your fart tax!"

Can't Pay the Fart Tax?

The old man was shaking from head to toe standing in front of Bobby.

"Please King Bobby, my family has farted all we can for you. We don't have any farts left. My family is all out of farts," the old man explained.

"All out of farts? There are always more farts, and you will give them to me now."

King Bobby stood up and walked towards the old man until he was standing over him.

"I know you have more farts in you and I know how to get them all out. Every single last fart. Guards, bring out the Flatulator!"

Flattened By the Flatulator...

The guards walked into another room. They came out from the darkness a few moments later wheeling in a giant contraption that looked like a giant rolling pin.

"Guards, put him through it. He will pay his fart tax one way or another." King Bobby declared.

"Please King Bobby," The old man pleaded, "please. I don't have any farts left. If I did I would give them to you. Don't put me through the Flatulator!"

But it was no use. The guards grabbed him and put him in front of the Flatulator. "Get me those farts!" said King Bobby.

They began to roll the machine over the old man from head to foot, flattening him like a pancake. By the end of it, the tiniest of poots escaped the man and was caught in a jar.

"I knew he was lying. There are always more farts. Now get him out of here." The guards scraped the old man off the ground with shovels and threw him into another room.

The Ancient Art of Fart-Fu

I saw the whole thing from the shadows, but I couldn't think of how to stop him in time. The poor old man never had a chance. It was over. The only thing that I could do now was to make sure that King Bobby never did something like this again.

Using the ancient teachings of Fart-Fu, I mustered up some gas. I focused my digestive tract and thought ninja star thoughts. Gas seeped slowly out of my butt and formed ninja fart-stars, which I got ready to throw. They may have been made of gas, but they were as solid as anything hand crafted by the ninjas themselves.

I made two and I knew that when I threw these, I could not miss. These stars had to fly true and had to hit their targets.

Ninja Farts to the Rescue!

I closed my eyes and focused on my throw to come. I opened my eyes and threw my ninja fart stars straight at King Bobby. They flew through the air leaving a gas trail behind them. My aim was good. The two fart stars each hit their target, one under each one of the evil king's nostrils.

"What's this?" The King yelled. "The smell! The smell is so bad! These are—these are the worst farts I've ever smelled in my life! With this power I could rule the world!"

The two stars exploded into a cloud of green gas with so much force that it knocked him over and he fell on his butt.

"These farts..." he mumbled before he passed out from the terrible smell. I knew that there was nobody—not even an evil king of farts—that could stand such a smell. The cloud around his head got bigger and bigger. This was the way of the ninja.

But Was it All a Dream?

All of a sudden my head felt like it was falling really fast towards a very hard surface that I really didn't want it to hit.

THWUNK. Oh man! I woke up from my dream because my head fell off my hand and slammed into my desk.

"Mr. Snotrocket," Mr. Figgins said, "now that you seem to be done sleeping, can you please tell me the answer to the question on the board?"

Oh boy. "Uhh," I said, "Can you repeat the question?"

Mr. Figgins sighed. "Mr. Snotrocket, can you please explain how I am supposed to repeat a question for you that is already written?" he asked.

I stammered something out, but didn't really say anything. All the other kids in class laughed at me. Man, I looked stupid.

What Would a Fart Ninja Do?

I was so disoriented that when the bell rang I could hardly believe that class was over. I guess I did accidentally sleep through just about the whole thing.

Oh well.

As I was putting my books into my backpack I saw something that made the hair on the back of my neck stand up: Bobby putting jars filled with green and yellow gas into his backpack. He was looking around, making sure nobody saw what he was doing and it looked like he thought he got away with it, but luckily I saw him.

What would a ninja do in this situation? What should *I* do? I think that a real ninja would fight for the forces of good and not allow a villain like this to get away with his evil plan. But I've only ever dreamt about being a ninja, I've never actually put the mask on and fought for good in real life before. I don't know if I can do it.

These thoughts bounced around my head like a pinball game being played by one angry kid.

Following Bobby Buttz-Cratcher

Well, at least for now, I should follow him I think. At least to see if Bobby's even going to go through with this plan after all. I mean, he might not even do it, so there would be no reason for me to become a ninja in the first place.

I followed him through the hallways, walking behind other kids, moving as they moved, stepped where they stepped. I became their shadow. I knew that if Bobby saw me following him I would be lucky if he only beat me up. It was a good thing I was so good at sneaking.

I guess if you spend enough time dreaming about being a ninja, you actually get pretty good at it. Cool huh?

Bottled Farts Are Pure Evil

Bobby stopped outside the girl's locker room, surrounded by his group of cronies.

"Hey Bobby, what do you got for us in there?" asked one of the group. They were all staring hungrily as Bobby took off his backpack and opened it so that the rest of the group could look inside. Bobby started laughing while he scratched his butt and showed off what he had.

"Check it out guys, I made this in science class. It's jarred farts. They smell way worse than anything that a person could fart out. Science rocks guys. You should really try harder so you can do this too."

I was watching this from behind a wall. What do I do here? A ninja would stop him.

"I'm going to open these and throw them into the girl's locker room. It's going to smell so bad and everybody will think that the girls all farted. It'll be the funniest thing that ever happened at this lame school and everyone's going to blame the girls. It's the perfect crime!"

Farts Are My Destiny...

I walked to the boy's locker room. It already smelled like farts in here. I walked up to my locker and opened it, revealing my ninja outfit.

I had been bringing it to school everyday for a year, just in case I ever had the courage to put it on and be a hero. A true hero would wear the mask and save the day, but I don't know if I am a true hero. Just dreaming about being a hero doesn't mean you are one.

A real hero is defined by their actions. They do heroic things because heroic things need to be done.

I'm not sure if I have that courage inside me.

I was terrified, but then I remembered something my dad once told me: "Courage is not having no fear, it is doing what is right even though you're scared."

Then I knew what I had to do. I took the costume out of my locker and became the fart ninja. I became the hero I needed to be. I became the hero that *everybody* needed me to be.

Bullies = No Match for Fart Fu

I came out of the boy's locker room. I emerged unnoticed by the other kids in the hall and snuck up behind Bobby. I got behind him and tapped him on the shoulder. He jumped and turned around.

"Who do you think you are, kid? Nobody touches Bobby Buttz-Cracher. Especially not some kid wearing stupid pajamas." he yelled. Then he pushed me in the chest. I didn't realize how much bigger he was than me until he was right in front of me, pushing me. I was about ready to pee in my ninja-pants...sneakily.

"I'm the fart ninja, Bobby. I am a master of Fart-Fu, and I know what you're planning to do. A real ninja would never let you get away with such an evil plan!" I said.

"Then it's a good thing there's not a real ninja around to try and stop me." He replied. Then him and all the kids around him started laughing.

"That is where you are wrong, Bobby. I am a real ninja, and no words can stop me from doing what's right. I will stop you, Bobby. I will stop you."

Merciful Farting

Then I focused all of my energy to my butt and let loose. A giant fart cloud erupted from me, blinding and gagging all of the kids around me. I made sure to hold back on the stinkiness so that none of the innocent witnesses were hurt.

I also made sure to make the fart extra thick so that no one saw as I rocketed up into the air on a fart jet. When I got to the ceiling I made an extra thick cloud out of farts and sat on it. I floated on it and figured out my next move.

Bobby was so much bigger and stronger than me. I had to remember everything I had learned, all of my ninja teachings.

Summoning the Ancient "Dragon Fart"

What was I taught? What is the ultimate ninja technique? Then it hit me. The single most powerful ninja technique that there is. I had to use it. I sat on my cloud and began to summon it.

I began a long series of farts, molding them into one being. I wove them together through the air, sticking them together in intricate and elaborate ways, creating a work of fart art. The great masters themselves could have made nothing more beautiful than what I had. Before I knew it, my masterpiece was complete.

 It was a giant dragon made of farts! It was the embodiment of all of the teachings of the ninja: silent, but deadly!

Horrible Farts Save the Day!

The dragon struck from the shadows. I sent it right at Bobby. If I missed, there was a chance that it could attack the wrong person. This dragon contained all of my ninja strength and was very difficult to control.

I mean, this thing was a **dragon**; it had a mind of its own. I could guide it, I could tell it what to do, but if it decided I was wrong or weak it would ignore me.

I gave it all of the information I could as I was making it and I trusted it to make the right choice and take down Bobby.

The dragon struck from the shadows, and it did the right thing.

It flew down and swallowed Bobby and his backpack full of farts up whole. It flew around the hallways until it farted out Bobby and his now empty backpack. All of the farts in Bobby's backpack had gotten out of their jars. The dragon turned Bobby and his jar of farts into its own fart, and farted him out.

Bobby was lying on the ground dazed. All of his hair had gotten burned off because of how bad the inside of the fart dragon smelled. All of the other kids covered their faces because they couldn't handle how bad Bobby smelled now.

An Important Speech About Farting

I jumped off of my fart cloud and walked over to Bobby, still lying on the ground.

"Bobby, I am very sorry that it came to this, but I had to stop you. You forced me to. You were using farts for the purposes of evil, but farts are supposed to be used for good. Farts are amazing, wonderful things.

"Everybody farts. Your mom farts, and your teachers fart and even girls fart. There is nobody on Earth right now who doesn't fart. To use farts for the purposes of evil makes something that we all do bad. It makes us all bad. If we use them for the forces of good, then we can make everybody better. We make the whole world better.

"Remember this Bobby, no matter how good you think you are at being evil, there will always be a fart ninja there to stop you. We defend the order of farts. We protect farts and the goodness that they all have in them. Some people say we're gross, and they might be right.

"In fact, forget the "might," they're completely 100% right. But we will do everything we can, to protect them."

Bobby stared up at me the whole time. His eyes even started to water and I don't think it was because of the smell.

A Bully Sees the Error of His Ways

Bobby started to talk, but at first it seemed like he was having some trouble getting all of the words out.

"I-I'm so sorry. It's just that because of my name, other kids used to make fun of me all the time...so I thought that the only thing that I could do to make them not make fun of me anymore was to bully them before they even had the chance.

"I don't want to be a bully! I'm just so scared that other kids are going to make fun of me, before they even get to know me. I'm really not a bad guy deep down. I just don't want other kids to hurt my feelings.

"I just thought that, since everybody likes farts so much, if I figured out how to make them then everybody would like me. I'm not a very good farter, but I'm really good at science. I'm really sorry. I just wanted to be one of the guys and fit in. But I guess I screwed up, and now everyone is going to make fun of me again."

Using Farts For Good...NOT For Evil

I had no idea that Bobby was such a complex person. I had assumed that he was a bully because he liked being mean. I guess even bullies are still just kids trying to be happy, just like the rest of us.

Bobby kept apologizing, over and over again. I held up a hand to stop him.

"Stop, Bobby. I'm the one who should be sorry. I underestimated you. I didn't give you a chance to prove that you were a good kid. Clearly you are, and because of that, I am going to make you an offer.

"Today I saw great fart potential in you. In fact, you have enough potential to join the ninja fart order. If you promise me that from now on you will only use your natural fart talent for the powers of good, I will train you."

I offered him my hand to help him stand up and get off the ground. He stood up and looked at me. His eyes were filling up with tears of joy.

"Thank you so much strange ninja! I swear I'll be good. You're right, farts are amazing and all I want to do is use them to make the world a better place for everyone! I'll train harder than anyone you ever met. I'll be the best fart ninja ever! Who are you?"

I took my mask off and looked at Bobby.

"You can call me Milo, friend."

Two Farts Are Better Than One!

Many months later, Bobby and I went out on a mission, two fart ninjas farting for the forces of good. There was a gang of bad guys smuggling farts across the border so that they could take down the government.

Bobby and I focused our power and created an army of fart dragons that flew through the air, who swallowed up the gang one at a time and farted them out. They all were so stunned by the smell that the police got there in time to put them all in jail, although they were pretty unhappy that they had to put so many stinky people into their cars.

"You know what Milo, we make a pretty good team." Bobby said.

"You know what Bobby, we really do."

A police officer came running up to us.

"Thank you so much young men. You two really are great warriors. You took down that whole gang." We thanked the officer for what he said. We really had gotten strong over the last few months. "

Who are you two? How did you do that so quickly?" He asked. Bobby and I looked at each other, and then responded at the same time:

"We're fart ninjas, fighting for the forces of good and for the purity of farts. We are ancient warriors in modern times, and we fight for good using nothing but our ninja farts."

MORE FUNNY FARTS...

If you laughed really hard at Ninja Farts, I know you'll love these other stinky bestselling books by J.B. O'Neil (for kids of *all* ages!)

http://jjsnip.com/fart-book

http://jjsnip.com/booger-fart-books

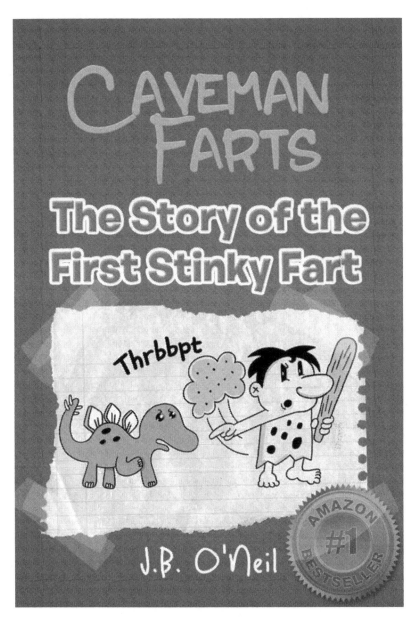

http://jjsnip.com/caveman-farts

A long time ago, in a galaxy fart, fart away...

http://jjsnip.com/fart-wars

http://jjsnip.com/dog-farts

And check out my new series, the

Family Avengers!

http://jjsnip.com/gvz

Made in the USA
San Bernardino, CA
04 November 2017